Songs of the Fog Maiden

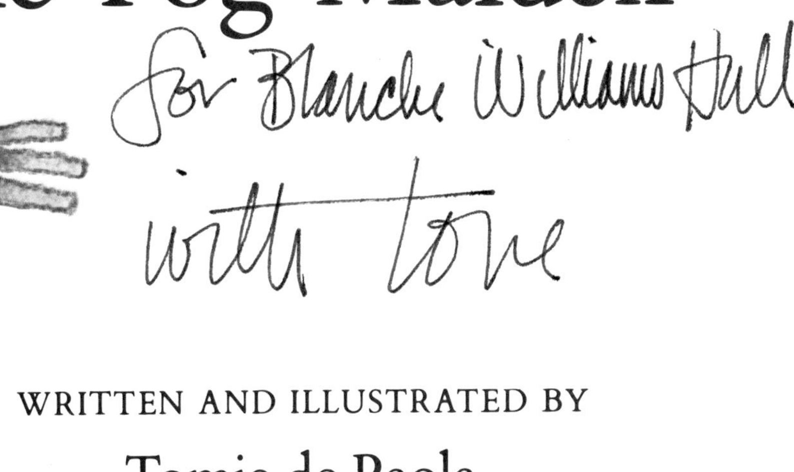

WRITTEN AND ILLUSTRATED BY

Tomie de Paola

Holiday House • New York

FOR MARGARET FRINGS
who shared the songs on a journey

Printed in the United States of America

Library of Congress Cataloging in Publication Data

De Paola, Thomas Anthony.
Songs of the fog maiden.

SUMMARY: The fog maiden sings her songs before and
after her nightly travels over the earth.
I. Title.
PZ7.D439So [E] 78-12822
ISBN 0-8234-0341-6

Somewhere,
between the Sun and the Cold,
lives the Fog Maiden.
Her castle sits high on a hill,
and outside the walls are two gardens.
There is a Day Garden and a Night Garden.

Every morning, when she returns from traveling over the Earth, the Fog Maiden opens the gate of her Day Garden, and she sings this song.

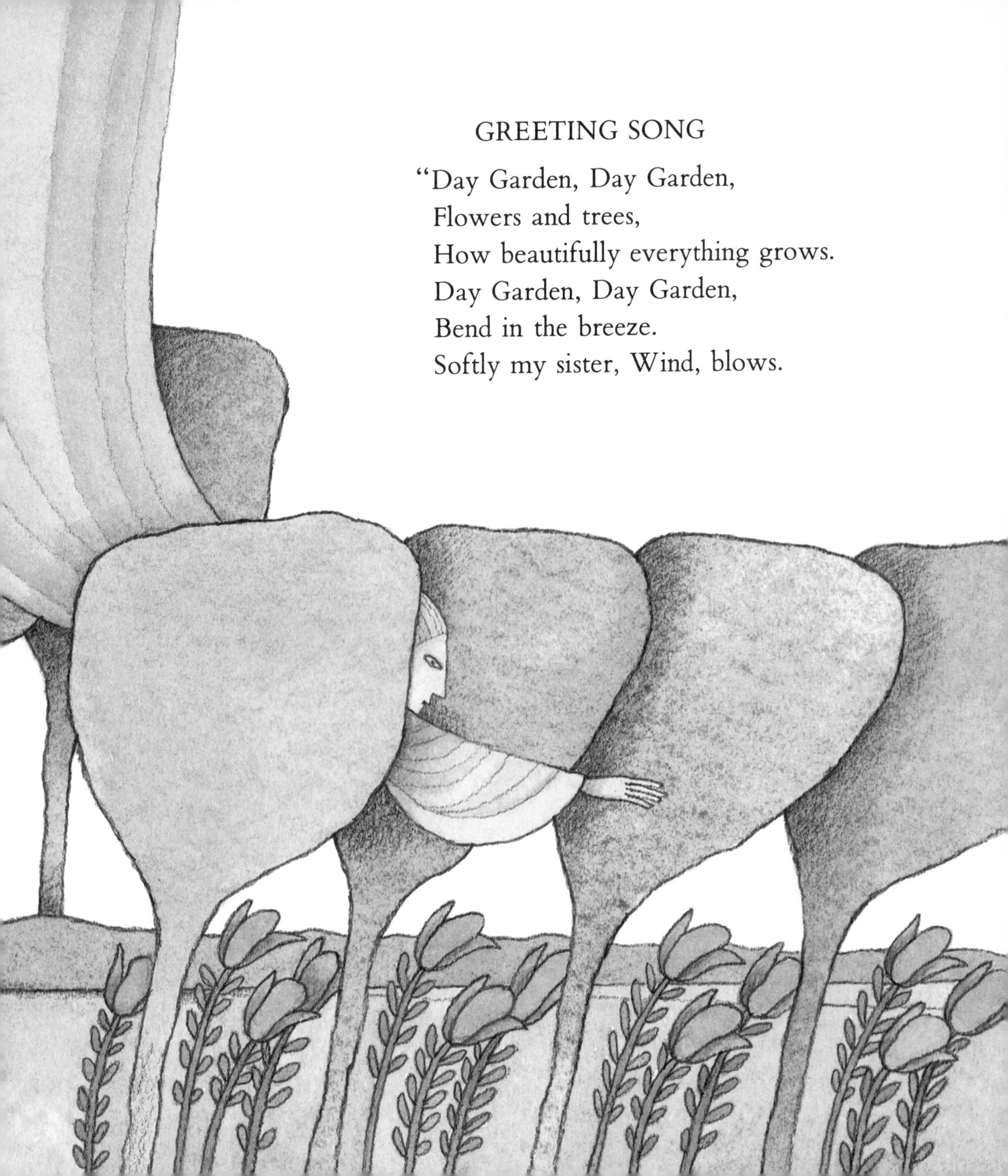

GREETING SONG

"Day Garden, Day Garden,
Flowers and trees,
How beautifully everything grows.
Day Garden, Day Garden,
Bend in the breeze.
Softly my sister, Wind, blows.

"Day Garden, Day Garden,
Filled with light,
A crystal fountain flows.
Day Garden, Day Garden,
Shining bright,
How beautifully everything grows."

There are rows and rows of statues
in the Day Garden.
The Fog Maiden sings to them, too.

STATUE SONG

"Statues, statues, everywhere,
Cats and birds and fish.
Statues, statues, everywhere,
Will I get my wish?

"Statues, statues, everywhere,
Do you dance and sing?
Statues, statues, standing there,
Knowing everything.

"Statues, statues, everywhere,
What shall my wish be?
Statues, statues, standing there,
I wish that you were free."

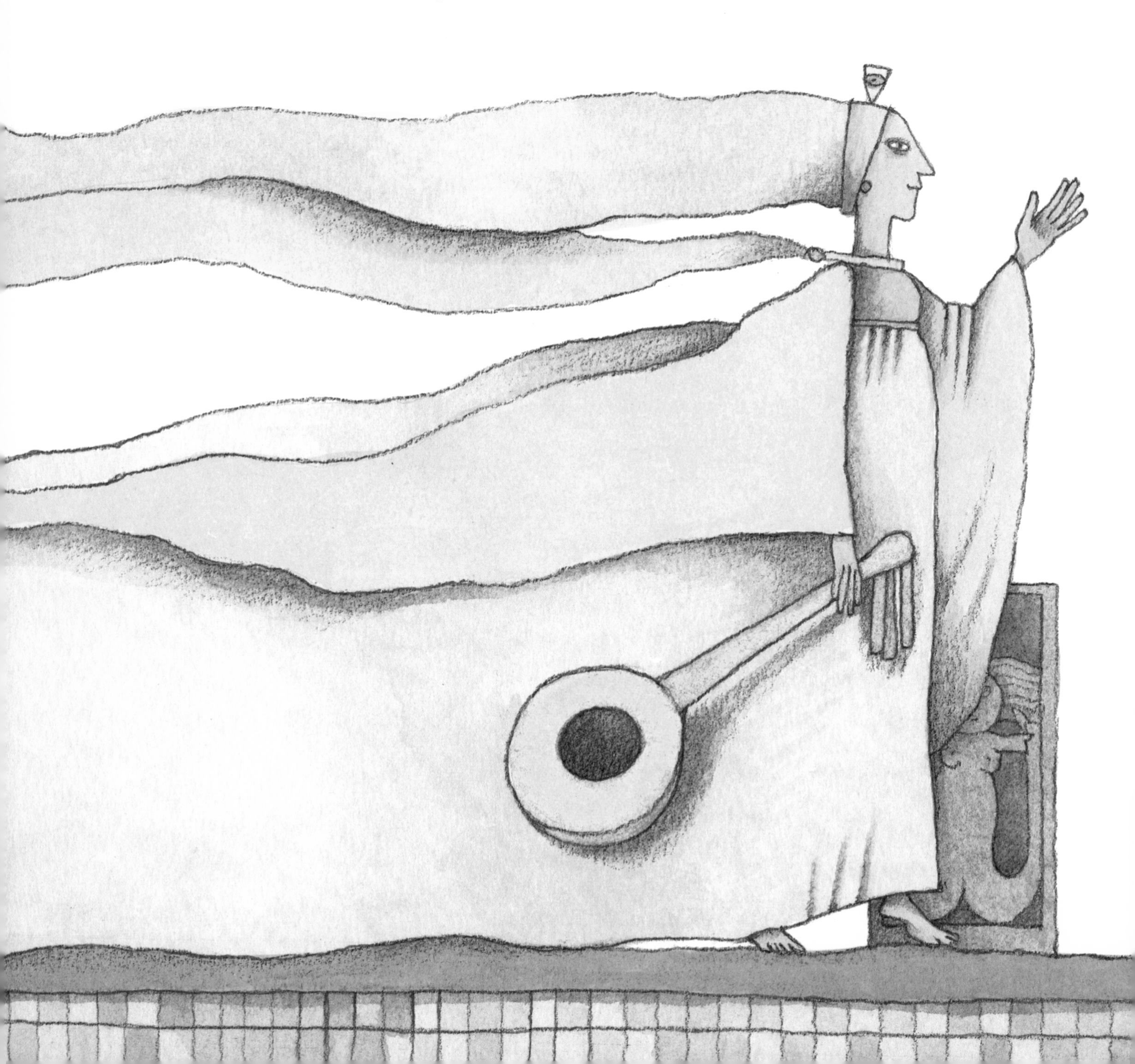

The Fog Maiden walks along the paths,
picking flowers as she goes.

WALKING SONG

"Paths that wander to and fro,
Paths that twist and turn,
All around my garden go,
Through flowers and through fern.

"Paths that find a secret place,
All shadowy and deep,
Where the sun can't show its face,
Here I'll stop and sleep."

The sun begins to set,
and it is time for the Fog Maiden
to leave her Day Garden.

LEAVING SONG

"Leaving, leaving, till tomorrow,
Flowers, nod your heads.
Time for yawning, time for sleeping,
Mothers turn down beds.

"Birds all flying to their branches,
It's the end of day.
Resting, resting, all are resting,
Night is on its way."

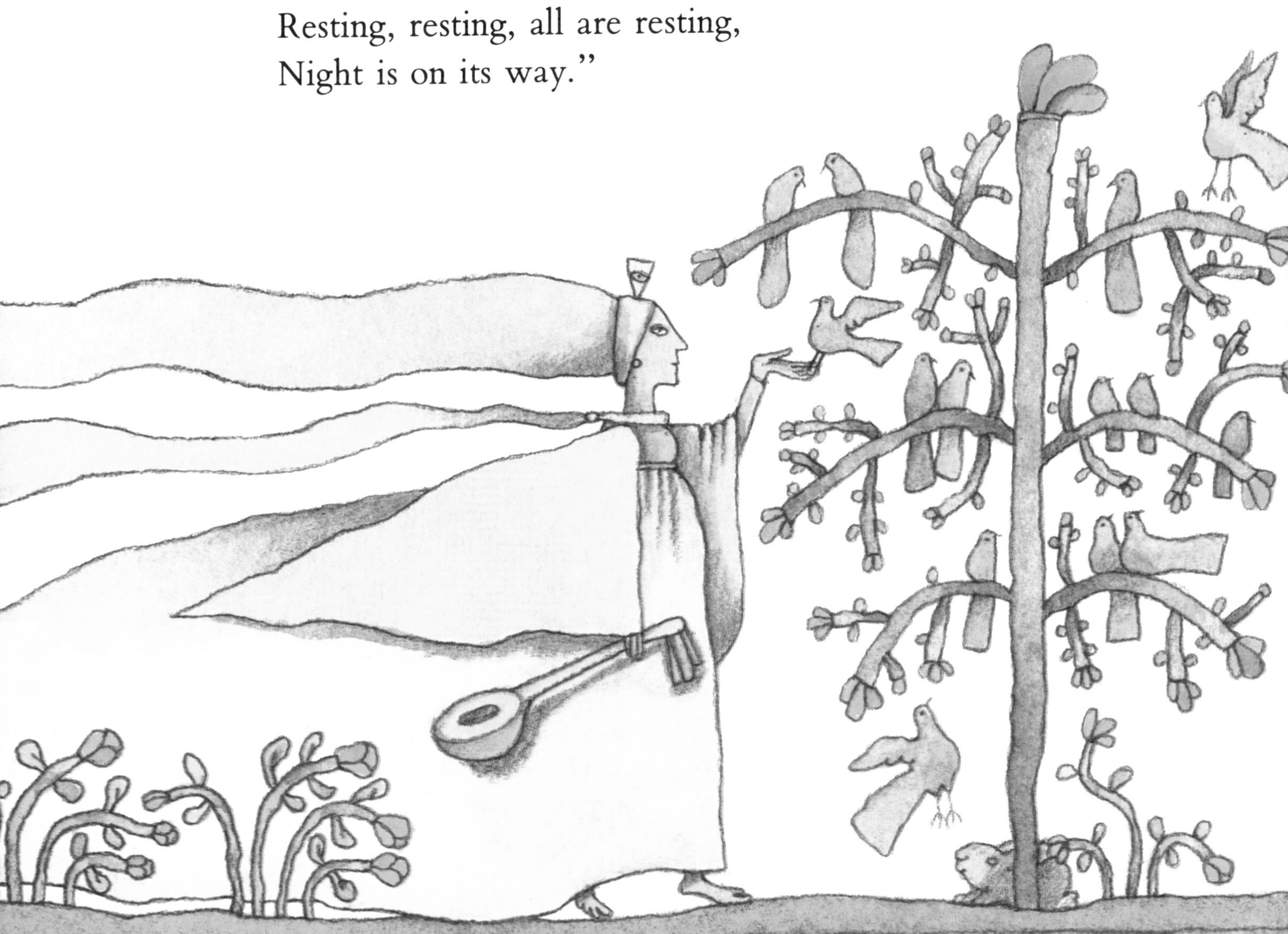

In the twilight, the Fog Maiden
opens the gate to the Night Garden.
Her cat, Token, comes out of the castle
to join her in a Night Garden walk.

NIGHT SONG

"The sun has set, the day is gone,
The stars must twinkle soon.
I'll throw some Star-Flowers in the sky,
And then I'll add a moon."

MOON-FLOWER SONG

"Which Moon-Flower will it be?
Thin, or big and round?
Which Moon-Flower will you see?
And will it make a sound?

"Listen closely, hear the song?
Moon-Flowers sing so dear.
Whooshing comets, whizzing by
Watch, so you will hear.

"Moon-Songs, Star-Songs, Night-Songs, too,
Come from far and near,
Tumbling gently from the sky.
The night is not to fear."

When the moon is high,
the Fog Maiden and Token visit the Earth.
The Fog Maiden covers everything
with her dress, and then she sings this song
to Token.

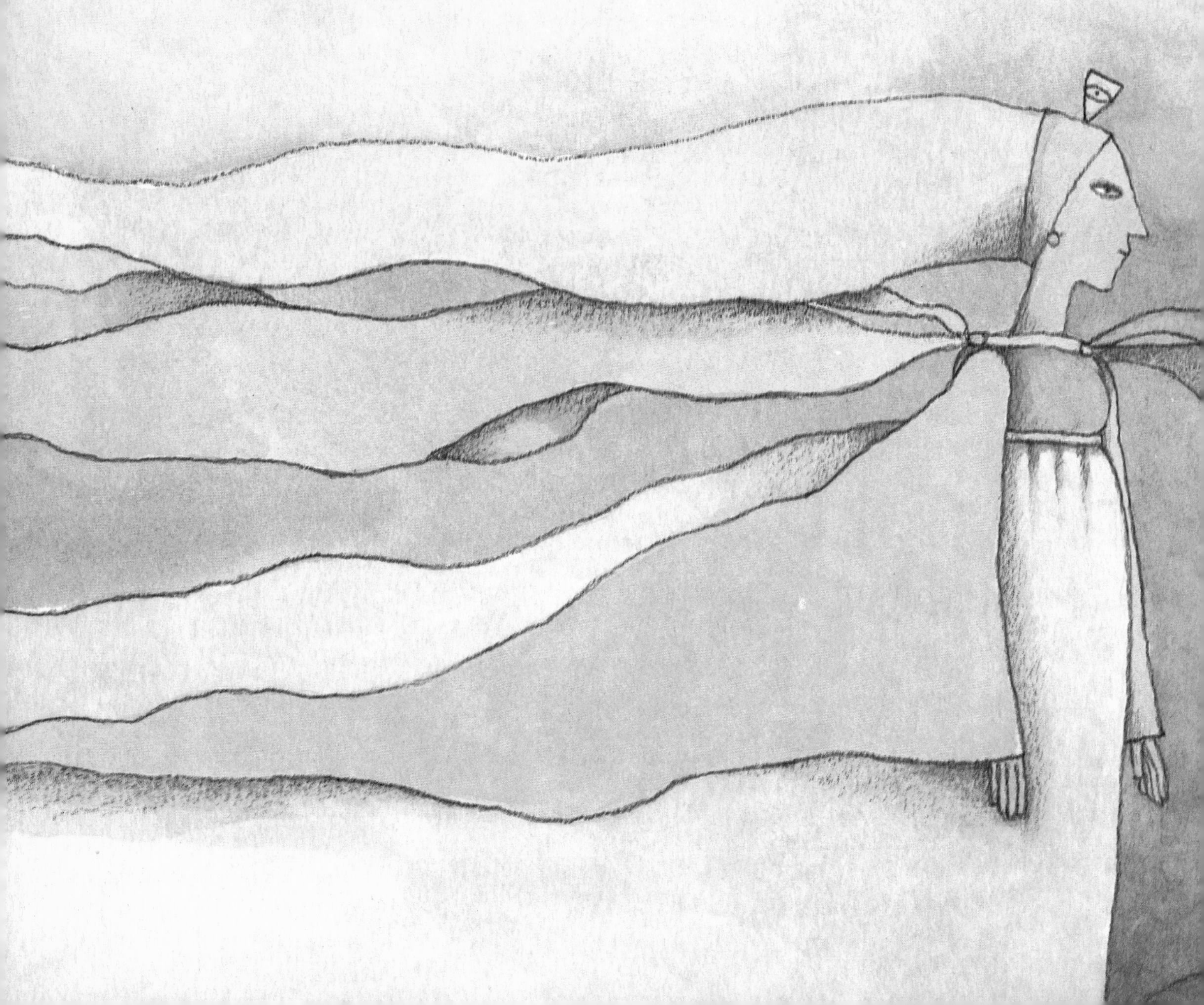

TOKEN'S SONG

"Token, Token, at the window,
Token, blue and fair.
Token, Token, at the window,
What do you do there?"

And Token sings back:

"I see children dreaming, fast asleep,
Till the stars begin to fade.
I watch and protect my sweet dear friends
So they'll never be afraid.

"I chase green goblins and nightmare-y things
Till they all run away and hide.
I whisper sweet dreams in the children's ears
And never leave their side.

"I'm Token the Cat, and I'm big and blue
And my feet never make a noise.
I watch and I purr and I stay here all night
To take care of the girls and boys."

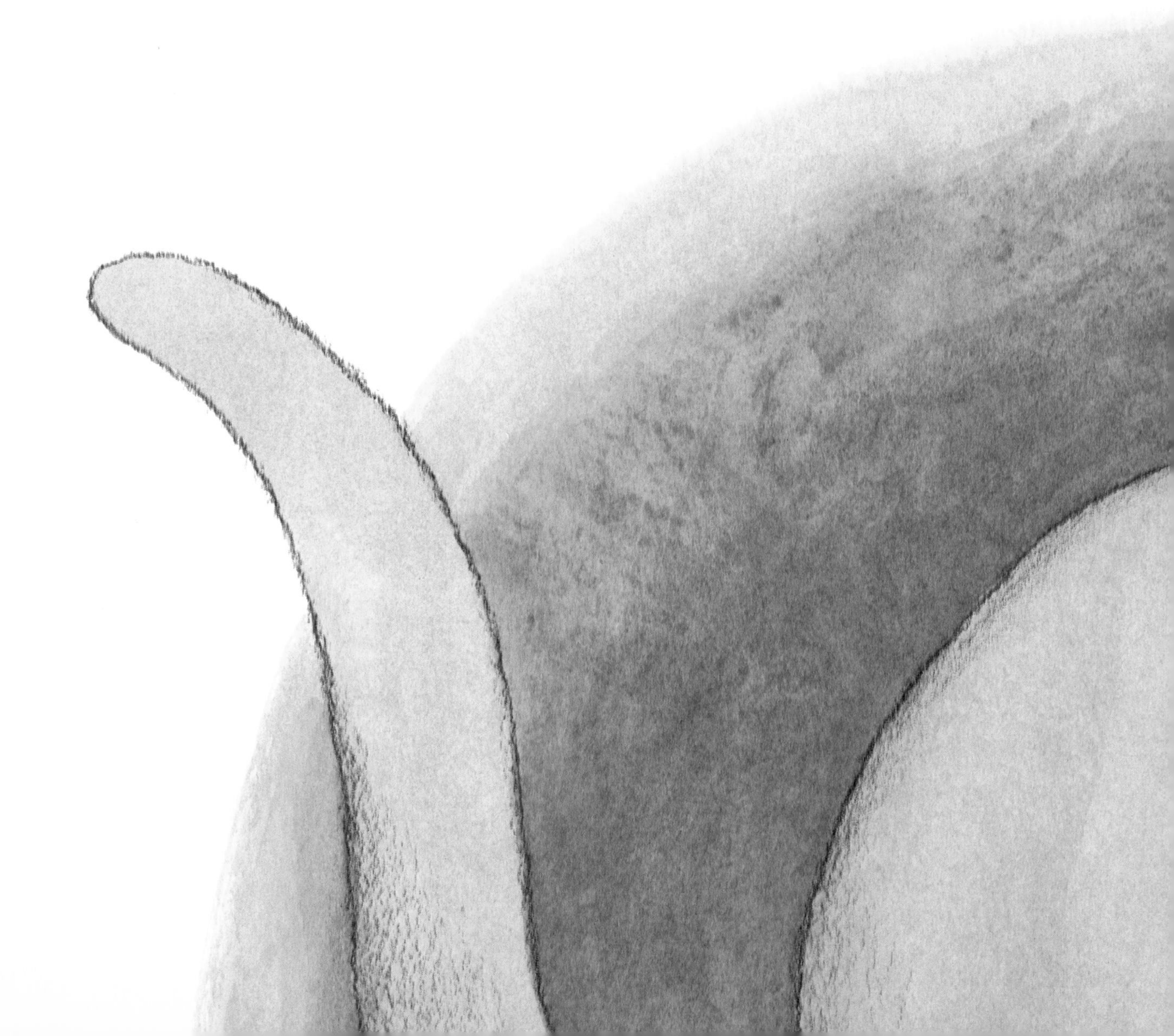

After the Moon has set
and before the Sun comes up,
the Fog Maiden gathers up her dress
to go home.

But before she leaves,
she and Token sing a song
to all the children of the world.

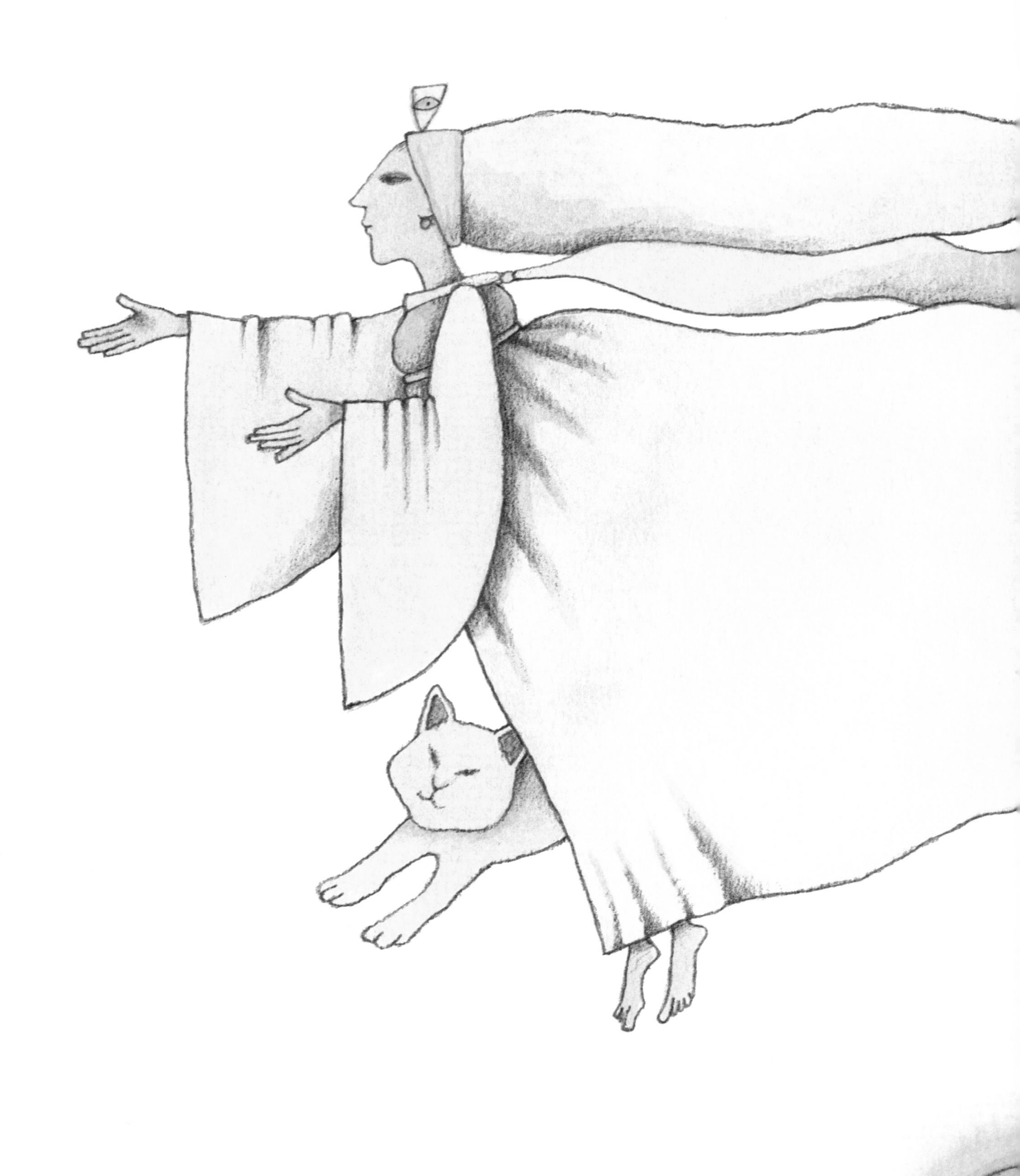

LOVE SONG

"Good night, sleep tight,
Soon the sun will rise.
Sleep tight, dream tight,
The morning bird now flies.

"Deep night, sweet night,
When you open your eyes,
No night, bright light,
The day is a new surprise."